Mr Johnson took his class away for the week. They went to a big house called Seabay House. Mrs May went too.

The children were excited. Seabay House was near the sea and there were lots of interesting things to do.

Everyone unloaded the bus.

"Some of these bags and cases are heavy," said Mr Johnson. "We're only here for a week."

Mrs May found a toothbrush. "Whose toothbrush is this?" she asked.

"Oh dear," said Biff. "I think it's mine."

Mr Johnson showed the boys their room.
"You'll be sleeping in here," he said.
"I want the top bunk," shouted Chip.
"No, I want the top bunk," shouted Wilf.
Mr Johnson tossed a coin.
"Heads or tails?" he said.

Mr Johnson gave the children a map. Then he took the children for a long walk. After a while they stopped for a rest.

The children looked at their maps. Mr Johnson showed them the places they could see.

"Your map's upside down, Biff," said Wilf.

Nadim pointed to a little island out at sea.

"What's that island called?" he asked.

"Look on your maps," said Mr Johnson.

"Who can tell me what the island is called."

Chip and Anneena knew.

"It's called Green Island," they said.

Everyone was hungry after the long walk.
When they got back it was time for supper.

The children served the food, and then they
helped wash up.

"I don't like washing up at home," said Wilf,
"but it's fun washing up here."

That night the children were tired but they couldn't sleep. Chip kept telling jokes and making silly noises.

In the end, Mr Johnson came in. He was cross with Chip.

"I'll send you to bed at six o'clock tomorrow, if I hear any more noise."

The next day, the children did a beach study.
Some children worked with Mr Johnson. They
made squares on the beach and looked at
everything in each square.

Biff found a shell with a crab inside it.

"It's called a hermit crab," she said.

Some children worked with Mrs May. They looked carefully in all the rock pools.

Nadim and Wilf caught a large crab.

"Look at this," they called.

Mrs May showed them how to hold the crab.

"We'll look at it, then we'll let it go," she said.

Chip and Anneena found a seagull. It couldn't fly.

"Oh dear!" said Mr Johnson. "It can't fly because it has oil on its feathers. Oil is hard to get off, so be careful, everyone. Mind you don't get oil on you."

"How do we get the oil off the seagull?" asked Chip.

Mr Johnson took the children to see Mrs Honey.

"If anyone can help the seagull, Mrs Honey can," said Mr Johnson.

"This poor old gull needs a clean," said Mrs Honey. She looked at Anneena and Chip. "And so do you," she said.

"Oil is terrible stuff," said Mrs Honey. "You can see what it does to animals and birds if it spills into the sea."

"It *is* terrible," said Mrs May. "I'm having trouble getting it off Chip and Anneena."

"I feel really sorry for the seagull," said Chip.

"What will happen to the seagull?" asked Wilf.

"It's feathers will be damaged," said Mrs Honey.
"So first we'll clean the oil off. Then we'll look
after it for a week or two. It has to get strong
again, and its feathers have to get better. Then
we'll let it go."

Mrs Honey looked after all kinds of animals.
She showed the children an otter. Then she gave
it some fish.

"She's a sea-otter," she said. "I call her Fiona.
She was hurt by a boat. Now she's better, I'm
going to let her go."

"Sea-otters live on Green Island," said
Mrs Honey. "If you like, you can come to the
island with me and watch me let Fiona go."

Mrs Honey had a boat.

"There's room for everyone," she said. "If we're
lucky, we may see some more sea-otters."

The children went across to Green Island in the boat. Mrs Honey stopped a little way from the island.

The children looked carefully. Suddenly Anneena pointed to some rocks.

"I can see another otter," she said. "Look, everyone."

"There aren't many sea-otters left!" said
Mrs May. "So that was a wonderful thing to see."
Mrs Honey let Fiona go. The otter dived into
the sea and swam towards the rocks.

"Will Fiona be all right now?" asked Wilf.
"I hope so," said Mrs Honey.

Mrs Honey took the boat to the other side of the island.

"You can get out, and explore," she said. "If you keep quiet, you will see all kinds of interesting sea birds."

The children jumped out of the boat and went to look around the island.

The children saw a small cave. They ran to
see it.

"I wonder if it has treasure in it," called Wilf.

"Maybe it's a secret tunnel," said Nadim.
"Maybe it leads to a secret computer base."

But when they got to the cave, they found
something else. In the cave were some drums.

"I don't like the look of this," said Mrs Honey.
"These drums have been dumped on Green Island.
They are full of toxic waste."

"Keep away from them, everyone," said Mr
Johnson.

"Why would anyone want to dump them here?"
asked Biff.

20

"It's hard to get rid of toxic waste," said Mrs May. "It costs a lot of money to do it safely. So people dump it."

"We should tell the police," said Mr Johnson.

"These drums can't stay here," said Mrs Honey. "They could do a lot of harm to the wildlife."

Suddenly, Chip and Wilf ran up to Mr Johnson.
"There's a boat coming to the island," said
Chip. "There are four people in it."

"I don't like the sound of this," said Mr Johnson.

"Keep out of sight, everyone," said Mrs Honey.
"I want to see what these people are doing."

The boat stopped at the island and four people got out. They lifted some drums out of the boat and began to carry them towards the cave.

"They're dumping more waste on the island," said Mrs Honey. "I want everyone to run back to my boat. Don't make a sound. I have an idea."

The children did what Mrs Honey told them.
They ran to the boat with Mrs May and
climbed in.

"I hope the boat will start," said Mrs May.
"If it doesn't, I don't know what we shall do."

"Do you think those people are dangerous?"
asked Chip.

Wilf and Chip pushed the boat out with the
oars and Mrs May started the engine.

"So far, so good," said Mrs May. "Let's hope
Mrs Honey's idea works."

"I hope Mrs Honey and Mr Johnson will be
all right," said Wilf.

Mrs Honey's idea worked. She and Mr Johnson had taken the other boat. The other people couldn't get off the island without it.

"Hooray!" shouted the children. "They won't get off Green Island unless they swim all the way back!"

"What are you doing with our boat?" shouted
a man. "Bring it back!"

"I'll get the police to bring it back," shouted
Mrs Honey. "You can tell them why you've dumped
toxic waste on Green Island."

"Grrr!" said the man.

The police took the people off the island.

"Taking their boat was a brilliant idea," said Mr Johnson.

"I'm glad we caught them," said Mrs Honey. "And I'm glad you were with me. I couldn't have taken their boat by myself."

"What an adventure!" said Mrs May.

"Look at those drums of toxic waste," said Wilf.
"I can't think why people would dump them
where they could do so much harm."

"I'm glad the otters will be safe on the island
now," said Anneena.

At the end of the week, there was a party.
Mrs May played her guitar and everyone sang
songs.

Mrs Honey came. She told the children stories
about some of the animals she had looked after.

"But you have the best story to tell," she said.
"It isn't every school trip that becomes famous!"

A photographer came. She made everyone
stand in a group. Then she took a photograph.

"We're going to be in the newspaper," said Wilf.
"We *are* going to be famous."

"I've never been famous before," said Chip.
"I wonder what it feels like."

Barking Echo

THURSDAY, 13 September

No. 1,445

35p

Kids save island from toxic time bomb

By Max Darby
Environment Correspondent

Quick thinking by animal-lover Harriet Honey and teacher Neville Johnson, with a group of primary school children, led to the dramatic arrest of four people found dumping drums of toxic waste on Green Island yesterday.

Mr Johnson, 39, with a group of fifteen children from the Ortree Primary School, Dagenham, had gone to the island to watch the release of a sea-otter looked after by Mrs Honey, 62, in her animal sanctuary near Pebble Bank.

The drama began when the children discovered drums of industrial waste in a cave on Green Island. Shortly afterwards, four people arrived on the island to dispose of more drums of waste.

In a commando-style operation, the children were taken safely off the island while their teachers confiscated the polluters' boat.

One of the children, Chip Robinson, 7, said, "It was exciting, but a bit scarey. We had to be really quiet while we got away from the island."

New home for Barking dogs

By Lauren Cassidy

Dagenham Borough Council has approved plan to build a new headquarte for the Barking Kennel Clu The two-storey structure w be located at the north-w corner of Dagenh Common, which will prov excellent walking facil for the dogs. The plans propose to double number of lamp posts i neighbouring streets.

Man hooks fish in garden p

By Felix Schon

His neighbours he was crazy, but fisherman George swore he saw a fi garden pond, that w a metre long, and proved his point b the creature, a piranha.

Mr Dovolil lives in Collar the fish ate scrap threw into the his house.

A man identified the fi South Americ piranha, which dumped in th

New engagement for Barking orchestra

By Amanda Harvey

It was revealed yesterday, that the Barking Symphony Orchestra has signed an agreement with Dagenham Borough Council to stage a series of outdoor concerts in the summer of next year. The borough's entertainment officer, Mr McArthur-Christie

Ronnie Barker opens school fête

By Aaron Jansen
Education Correspondent

The well known comedian and actor Ronnie Barker, 61, officially opened this year's Garden Fête in the grounds of Ortree Primary School last Saturday. Among the celebrities attending were Rod Hunt, 45, the famous author and Alex Brychta, a popular children's book illustrator.

During their visit, the pair entertained children by writing and illustrating a book which will be on permanent display at the school.

Before departing, Mr Hunt said, "We've had a wonderful time. I feel as if I've known these children all my life."

children, Wilma Brown, 8, presented Mr Ortree School's own

Barking woman wins at dog show

By Pat Pilgrim

The Dagenham Dog and Cat Show raffle was won by Miss Emily Bell of 22 Winalot Drive, Barking. The prize, a year's supply of doggie choc drops, was donated by the Barking Kennel Club. Miss Bell, 18, a former pupil of Ortree Comprehensive School said, "I only came along with my boyfriend,

---

The next day the story of Green Island was in the newspaper. The children were excited.

"I'm going to buy three newspapers," said Chip.

"One for me, one for Mum and Dad, and one for Gran."

"Now I'm famous I don't feel any different," said Wilf.